Woody
The Kentucky Wiener

A New Home

by

Leigh Anne Florence

Illustrations by James Asher

International Standard Book Number 0-9741417-2-0
Library of Congress Card Catalog Number 2005920540

Cover design and book layout by Asher Graphics
Illustrations by James Asher

Manufactured in the United States of America

All book order correspondence should be addressed to:

HotDiggetyDog Press
P.O. Box 747
Shepherdsville, KY 40165

502-376-5966
leighanne@thewoodybooks.com
www.thewoodybooks.com

*This book is dedicated to my brother,
Guy Furr, for giving me the
sweetest gift ever—
a beautiful little redheaded
miniature-dachshund named Chloe.*

Special Thanks from Leigh Anne

First, as always, to my husband Ron. Being married to you and getting
to work with you and the puppies everyday is such a joy. I couldn't, nor wouldn't,
do this without you. Any man who works and travels with his wife and
two wiener dogs certainly deserves the "Husband of a Lifetime" Achievement Award!
I love you so much!

To each of you who has influenced my life. Whether it be my family, my closest
friends, the talented team at McClanahan, or someone I have met along this
incredible journey, you have certainly made an imprint on my heart.
I am thankful our paths have crossed. Thank you for supporting me, encouraging
me, and for falling in love with Woody and Chloe over and over again.

And finally, to my sweet, sweet puppies, Chloe and Woody. You mean the world
to me. Thank you for showing me what unconditional love and patience is all about.
Being your Mommy is the best! I love both of you more than you will ever know!

In Tinytown, Kentucky
Is a family of four —
With a Mommy
and a Daddy,
And two puppies
they adore.

Woody is a wiener dog -
A funny little man,

With a long and skinny body
And a coat of black and tan.

Chloe is his sister –
The older of the pair.

She is such a pretty puppy
With brown eyes and dark red hair.

They spend their time together
Where they laugh and romp and roam,
Enjoying everyday
In a place they call their home.

The four are very thankful,
Time and time again,
For they are more than just a family
They are the best of friends.

Chloe loves to daydream
And look up at the sky.
Woody loves to run and play,
Chase balls and butterflies.

Sometimes they have picnics
And share goodies Mommy made.
Sometimes they play checkers
And sit under the shade.

"Let's play cards!" said Woody
On one lazy summer day.
"Do you want to play Go Fish
or would you rather play Old Maid?"

"That sounds fun," said Chloe
"But since it's such a pretty day
Let's go take a walk
And pick flowers on the way."

"Great idea!" said Mommy
"Let's hurry up and go!
But first come here sweet puppies,
There is something you should know."
The pups both followed their parents,
Then Woody turned so pale
When he finally saw the sign
With the words that said "FOR SALE."

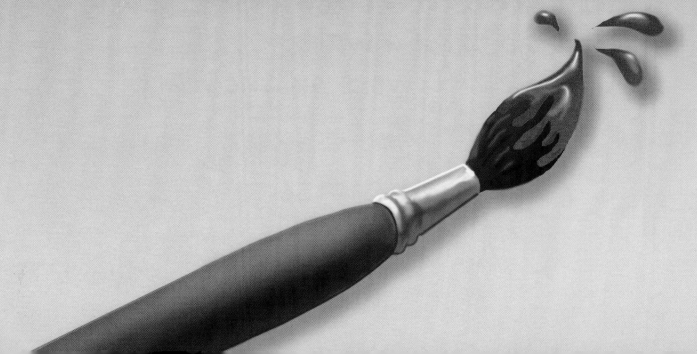

"I can't believe it Chloe!"
Woody looked so scared and lost.
"I wonder why they are selling us?
And HOW MUCH DO WE COST?

CHECKERS

Chloe   Woody

TOYS

I never thought this would happen.
Mommy, tell me it's not true!
Are you selling me and Chloe?
Or are you selling Daddy too!"
Mommy, Daddy, and Chloe
Laughed with all their might,
Then Mommy picked up Woody
And kissed and held him tight.

"I love you," whispered Mommy
As quietly as a mouse.
"We would never sell you or Chloe,
What we're selling is our house!"

"Oh thank Goodness!" said Woody
As relief began to show.
"But what's wrong with our house?
And now where will we go?"

"I want to know," said Chloe
"If we will have a place to play.
Will we make new friends?
Will Santa find his way?"

"No need to worry puppies!"
Daddy said so tenderly.
"We know you are going to love it!
Just you wait and see!

We are moving to the country,
With lots of trees and land.
There is even a big lake to fish,
We know you'll think it's grand.

Of course you'll make new friends!
You have so much to give.
And don't you worry
          about ol' Santa Claus,
He'll know where you live!

We know you may be scared,
But don't worry or feel blue.
It's not a house that makes a home —
It's spending time with you!"

The four shared a hug —
Woody and Chloe smiled with joy!
Then they hurried in the house
To start packing up their toys!